Hau Kea
and
The Seven Menehune

By Donivee Martin Laird
Illustrated by Carol Ann Jossem

Barnaby Books   Honolulu, Hawaii

Also by Barnaby Books
The Three Little Hawaiian Pigs and the Magic Shark
  (The Three Little Pigs)
Keaka and the Liliko'i Vine
  (Jack and the Beanstalk)
Wili Wai Kula and the Three Mongooses
  (Goldilocks and the Three Bears)
'Ula Li'i and the Magic Shark
  (Little Red Riding Hood)

Published by:
Barnaby Books - a Hawaii Partnership
3290 Pacific Heights Road
Honolulu, Hawaii 96813

Printed and bound in Hong Kong under the direction of
KWA Communications, Inc. (808) 536-4255

Library of Congress Catalogue Number: 95 - 077136
ISBN 0-940350-26-2

For Custard,
the very best mongoose in the world,
and Charlie who asked,
"When are you going to write another book?"

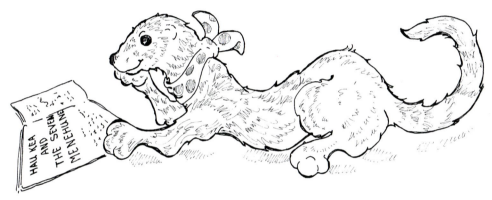

PRONUNCIATION GUIDE

The 12 letters in the Hawaiian alphabet are:

A, E, H, I, K, L, M, N, O, P, U, W

consonants

H, K, L, M, N, P are pronounced as in English

W is usually pronounced as V

vowels

A like a in farm

E like e in set

I like y in pretty

O like o in hold

U like oo in soon

plural

As there is no S in Hawaiian, the plural is formed by word usage or the addition of another word such as na to the sentence.

THE LANGUAGE SPOKEN BY THE MENEHUNE IS PIDGIN ENGLISH
IN USING THIS DIALECT, THE AUTHOR HAS NO WISH TO OFFEND ANYONE,
BUT ONLY TO SHARE THE SPECIAL FLAVOR PIDGIN ENGLISH ADDS TO HAWAI'I.

Once upon a time, deep in a secret valley in the Ko'olau Mountains there lived seven Menehune brothers. Their names were Hilahila, Molohai, Huhu, Akamai, Hanabata, Hau'oli and Gecko.

The brothers lived in a tiny stone hale beside a noisy, rushing stream. Each evening, just as the sun was slipping into the sunset-colored ocean, they set off for work carrying their 'o'o, hammers, buckets and kaukau tins full of food. They walked to other valleys or to the lowlands to build walls, dig ditches and make fish ponds. Menehune, who see well in the dark, always work at night. Long hours later, as the sun came up out of the eastern ocean, and the sky began to grow pale, they were on the path home, hungry, dirty and very tired.

Each morning they washed in their stream, cooked and ate their supper, cleaned their house, and tended their garden. Then, they slept the day away. Over and over the pattern repeated itself, for Menehune did not know about weekends or holidays. Once in a while they would look sadly at their musical instruments. Remembering when they were young and carefree, they longed for time to sing and play.

In a village near the seashore there lived an evil queen, Wailuna, who believed she was the most beautiful woman in all the land. Her 'aumakua was a pueo, the Hawaiian short-eared owl. This pueo was devoted to his mistress.

Each day Wailuna went to her favorite pond and admired her reflection. The pueo watched from a branch nearby.

The queen always asked the same question:

"Pueo, pueo so very wise
Who is the fairest one of them all?"

The Pueo would always answer:
        "Queen, Queen, fair Queen,
        By me the truth is seen.
        What I speak is always true.
        The most beautiful is you."
    This delighted Wailuna. She knew
her 'aumakua was very wise and that a pueo
would never tell a lie.

One warm summer day Queen Wailuna sat beside the pond gazing at herself. After a while she asked her question: "Pueo, pueo so very wise

Who is the fairest one of them all?"

To her shock, the pueo answered:

"Queen, Queen, fair Queen,

By me the truth is seen.

Rival beauty there is I fear

In one villagers of Nu'uanu hold dear."

The queen leapt to her feet and screeched furiously. "It cannot be! I am the fairest, no one else is fairer than I. Go, find this maiden. Then return and tell me what you see. E 'awiki mai 'oe!"

The pueo flew to the valley called Nu'uanu. A helpful Kolea bird knew at once who the queen's 'aumakua was looking for. "Ah, Hau Kea," he said. "She is there picking 'ilima for her mother."

The pueo watched Hau Kea. The girl's skin was white, like snow. Her hair was as black as the feathers of the 'alala. She moved like a graceful leaf, blowing in the breeze. Her voice was soft and warm; her laughter was like gentle music.

Inside and out she truly was the loveliest in the land.

When he returned to Wailuna, the pueo reported, "I saw the girl and I cannot tell a lie. She is truly the loveliest in the land." The owl got a soft look in his evil eyes. "Her skin is so white, her hair so black; she has such grace, is so kind." At the look on Wailuna's face, he stopped and then quickly said, "She is the hanai child of a village woman. Her father, a ship captain, and her mother were lost at sea on a whaling voyage."

"They should have taken her with them," said Wailuna in a cold, evil voice. "For I and only I must be the loveliest."

The queen began to plan ways to get rid of Hau Kea. When she thought of Hau Kea's beauty, she became so upset that she would shriek and stomp in fury. Her anger made the villagers shake with fear.

Now it happened that a friend of Hau Kea's aunty was visiting a friend of hers whose cousin lived near the queen. And so, with talking and gossiping, the information that Wailuna wished to destroy Hau Kea came to the ears of her hanai mother.

Early the next morning, the mother woke Hau Kea. "Come my darling child, you are in great danger. The queen, Wailuna, plans to kill you," she explained. "Luckily, a kind hunter has offered to help. He will take you far into the mountains."

"There is much to eat in the valleys, and the streams are clear and fresh. You will be safe. When Wailuna has forgotten, I will come to find you. Go now." She handed a bundle of food and clothing to the frightened girl and pushed her gently towards the hunter.

Wailuna was sure that word of her anger would soon travel to Hau Kea's village, so she sent a hunter to Nuʻuanu and ordered him to offer to take the girl into the mountains should she try to flee. Once they were deep in one of the valleys he was to kill Hau Kea. To prove that she had died, Wailuna demanded that the hunter bring Hau Kea's heart back with him.

Together the girl and the hunter hiked for many miles. At a place where two paths met, the hunter stopped. "Run quickly, little one, up that way. E ʻawiki mai ʻoe!" he urged. As he turned away, he whispered, "You are too lovely to kill."

Terrified, Hau Kea ran as fast as she could.

Before he left the mountains, the hunter killed a wild boar and cut its heart out. He wrapped the heart in some ti leaves and took it to the wicked queen. Thinking it was Hau Kea's heart, Wailuna was satisfied.

Hau Kea went deeper and deeper into the mountains. She climbed steep ridges and then slipped and slid down their other sides into valley after valley. After many hours, the sun was disappearing into the western sea and Hau Kea was very tired. She came to a clearing where she saw a small hale. "How cute," she thought as she peeked in the open door. No one was at home.

Hau Kea stepped inside and looked around. There were seven little beds all in a row, each with its own colorful quilt. There were seven hooks on the wall, each with a hat hanging on it. Scattered inside the door were seven pairs of house slippers. In the center of the room was a tiny table with seven chairs set around it. On the table were seven cups and seven bowls. A large calabash, full of food and covered with cool ti leaves, was waiting for the owners to return. Hau Kea nibbled a piece of 'ulu and a slice of papaya. More than being hungry, she was very tired and wanted to rest, just for a moment. She curled up on one of the beds and was soon sound asleep, never noticing that the night passed swiftly by.

When it was nearly dawn, the seven brothers were over the ridge and down in another valley. They put the last few rocks in the wall they just finished. Hoisting their equipment and empty kaukau tins over their shoulders, the seven weary men marched home.

At the door of their little hale they stopped in surprise.

"Eh, Akamai," said the first man, whose name was Huhu. "Try look. One wahine stay on top my bed."

Akamai walked in the house and right behind him crowded the others. "Yes," said Akamai. "It looks like a girl on your bed."

"I like see," whispered Hau'oli trying to peek around Hilahila who was too shy to enter the hale.

"So, what you going do?" shouted Huhu.

With a start Hau Kea awoke. "Oh, dear, I fell asleep. I'm - I'm sorry." She sat up, rubbed her eyes and looked around in amazement. "Menehune!" she gasped.

"Who are you?" asked Akamai.

"What you stay doing on top my bed?" Huhu demanded in a loud voice.

"I like see," came Hau'oli's voice again.

"I am Hau Kea," she replied and tears rose in her eyes. "I have been sent away to the forest to escape a wicked queen named Wailuna."

"Fo' real?" asked Hanabata, wiping his nose.

"What you wen do?" asked Molohai in a most sleepy voice.

"I don't know," sighed the girl. "My mother said it's because I am pretty."

"Dat no bulai!" whispered Gecko.

"I like see!" demanded Hau'oli as he pushed Hilahila through the door. Hilahila was so embarrassed he dove under the bed and refused to come out for many hours.

Hau Kea told her story. The seven men listened. When the story was finished, everyone looked very sober.

The Menehune spoke softly and quickly to one another. Then Akamai said, "If you will take care of our hale and cook for us while we are at work, you may stay here."

"Oh," cried Hau Kea, clapping her hands.
"Yes. Yes. Yes!"
She was so excited that she kissed
each man on top of his head.
All, that is, except Hilahila
who was still hiding
under the bed.

Hau Kea stayed with the Menehune and their life settled into a gentle routine. Each evening the men set off to work. While they were gone, Hau Kea cooked and cleaned. When they returned at dawn, the hale was neat and the meal warm and ready. The Menehune were delighted.

Best of all, at last there was time for music. Out came the dusty instruments; they were tuned, and soon singing and laughter filled everyone's heart.

Akamai warned Hau Kea to stay indoors out of sight. "When you go outside, wear one of our hats low over your face. Wailuna may send her 'aumakua looking for you."

"Eh," Molohai always added, "No talk to no strangahs."

Back at her pond, the queen continued to ask her question and to hear the answer she wanted until one day she asked:

"Pueo, pueo so very wise
Who is the fairest one of them all?"

The pueo answered:
"Queen, Queen, fair Queen
By me the truth is seen.
In the mountains where Menehune dwell,
Hau Kea is alive and well.
You may be as lovely as the sun
But Hau Kea is the lovelier one."

The queen turned purple and then orange with rage. She had been tricked. Hau Kea was still alive. Furiously the queen stomped and paced and planned until she had an idea.

"Come," she called to the pueo. "We go to the forest."

The pueo flew ahead, leading the way to the little stone hale. Disguised as an old woman, Wailuna carried a basket of fruit over her arm. She carefully placed a large yellow guava on the top of the pile. It looked delicious but was full of *poison*.

"Aloha," she called in a sweet voice as she stepped into the clearing.

Hau Kea peeked timidly from the little hale. "Who are you?" she asked in a shaking voice.

"Only a kupuna hot and tired from walking and picking fruit for my darling mo'opuna," came the answer. "May I drink from your stream?"

"Oh!" cried Hau Kea much relieved. "Of course." She watched as the old woman drank greedily.

When the woman stood to leave, she called towards Hau Kea, "I leave this guava as a mahalo. It is ready to eat today."

"No! No!" exclaimed Hau Kea. "There is no need." However the woman was gone and the large yellow guava was left behind.

Very cautiously Hau Kea poked her head out the door; she looked around but could see no one. The guava looked delicious. She put one of the Menehune's hats on and took a step outside. She stopped and looked around again. There was no one in sight. Then she took one more step and then another and another until she was right beside the guava. She picked it up and smelled it. She didn't notice that all the birds and forest creatures were quiet. They knew who the old woman was and of the danger to Hau Kea, but there was nothing they could do.

Hau Kea smiled and took a large bite of the luscious fruit. She was still smiling as she collapsed and fell to the ground - dead.

"At last," said the queen from her hiding place. "She is dead."

Now, as evil as the pueo was, there was just a tiny speck of goodness left in him. When the queen had disappeared down the path, the bird flew back and landed on the dead girl. Using all of his powers he chanted:

"Poison, poison, stop; do not kill
Instead, in sleep let Hau Kea be forever still."

Then off he flew.

That evening, when the Menehune came home, they found Hau Kea lying beside the stream, the guava in her hand.

"Awe! Plenty pilikia," said Huhu. "She stay make."

"Da queen! Da ugly queen. I like show dat dirty buggah!" shouted Hilahila, no longer shy.

"Try wait," cried Molohai. "She stay bre'ting. Da skin, she stay wa'm."

The Menehune gathered around Hau Kea, touching her skin, watching her breathe.

"She stay make moemoe," whispered Hau'oli.

"She no make?" shouted Gecko, grabbing her arm. "Wake 'em up!"

They shook her, called to her, tickled her and pinched her softly, ...but nothing worked.

Finally the Menehune carried Hau Kea indoors and gently placed her on a bed.

They combed her hair and bathed her face, hands and feet, begging her to wake up as they worked, but Hau Kea continued to sleep.

The Menehune did not go to work for many days. Instead, they built a small stone hale for Hau Kea beside their own. They placed her upon a pune'e made of koa wood, covering her with a kapa so beautiful it shimmered in the light. Each morning the Menehune cleaned the tiny hale and bathed the maiden. She looked as fresh and lovely as she was the moment she took the bite out of the guava.

Back at her stream the queen asked:
"Pueo, pueo so very wise
Who is the fairest one of them all?"
The pueo answered truthfully:
"Queen, Queen, fair Queen,
By me the truth is seen.
Hau Kea sleeps. It is done.
You are now the fairest one."
The queen was pleased.

A few months later, the king of Kaua'i came from his island to visit the king of O'ahu. With him he brought his handsome son. The young man, growing tired of talking and visiting, decided to explore the mountains. As he hiked, the way became steep. He climbed up ridges and then slipped and slid down their other sides into valley after valley. As the day grew to an end, he stopped at a stream for a drink. He noticed two stone hale.

He looked in one. He saw seven beds, seven hats, seven pairs of house slippers, seven chairs and seven bowls. "A place I can sleep tonight," he thought, for it was nearly dark.

When he looked in the other hale, he saw a beautiful maiden and instantly fell in love with her. "She must be my wife," he thought as he tried to wake her. Nothing happened.

Again and again he tried, but she did not stir. Through the night he sat at her side, holding her hand, looking at her lovely face, talking to her and continuing to hope she would awaken.

When the Menehune came home the next morning, they discovered the young man. They explained why Hau Kea could not be awakened.

"I love her. Let me take her with me," he begged. "I will pay whatever you wish."

They saw how much the young man loved her. Gathering closely together, they talked.

Turning to the prince, Akamai spoke, "You may take her to Kaua'i; then Wailuna will never know she lives in sleep," he said. "We want no payment. We ask only that we may kiss her goodbye."

One by one the Menehune gently kissed Hau Kea's soft cheek. When they were finished, the young man added his kiss.

Hau Kea's eyes fluttered and opened. She was awake. The spell of the pueo was no match for the kisses of eight true loves.

What happiness! "It's party time!" cried Gecko and Hau'oli together.

"No," cautioned Akamai. "The queen might find out and come after Hau Kea. The prince must take her to Kaua'i tonight."

Plans were made to slip into the prince's canoe during the night. The Menehune were very sad that Hau Kea was leaving, but knew for her safety, she must go.

"Auwe," sighed Hau'oli, not feeling happy. "I going miss dat wahine."

Hilahila nodded. "Make my eye wata."

"Mo' betta dis way," sighed Huhu. "Bumbye dat ugly buggah Wailuna she come."

Hau Kea was happy to be going with the prince for she loved him as much as he loved her. At the same time she was sad to be leaving the seven Menehune. The prince couldn't bear seeing his beloved unhappy even for a moment.

"Akamai, come with us," the prince invited. "There is much work for Menehune on Kaua'i, and we need you."

Akamai looked at his brothers. They all grinned and nodded. Molohai shouted, "We go!" Hau Kea was so excited she hugged everyone except Hilahila who hid.

Late that night Hau Kea, the prince, and the seven Menehune slipped out of the mountains to a boat landing far from the wicked queen's village. A large double hulled canoe awaited them. When everyone was safely aboard, they set sail to the north. The boat left Oʻahu behind and sounds of happy music and singing could be heard floating over the gentle sea. The celebration had begun.

GLOSSARY

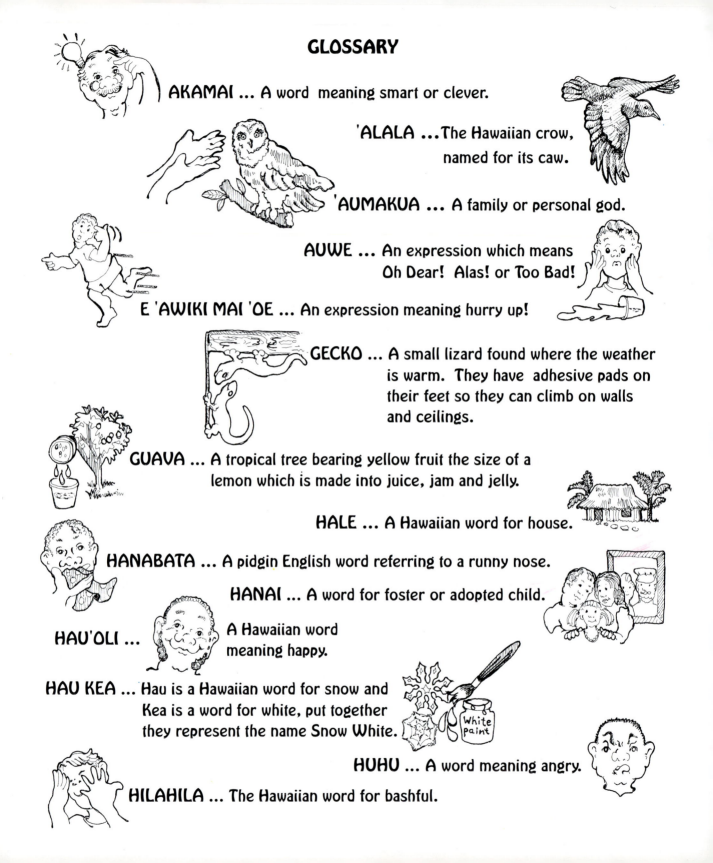

AKAMAI ... A word meaning smart or clever.

'ALALA ... The Hawaiian crow, named for its caw.

'AUMAKUA ... A family or personal god.

AUWE ... An expression which means Oh Dear! Alas! or Too Bad!

E 'AWIKI MAI 'OE ... An expression meaning hurry up!

GECKO ... A small lizard found where the weather is warm. They have adhesive pads on their feet so they can climb on walls and ceilings.

GUAVA ... A tropical tree bearing yellow fruit the size of a lemon which is made into juice, jam and jelly.

HALE ... A Hawaiian word for house.

HANABATA ... A pidgin English word referring to a runny nose.

HANAI ... A word for foster or adopted child.

HAU'OLI ... A Hawaiian word meaning happy.

HAU KEA ... Hau is a Hawaiian word for snow and Kea is a word for white, put together they represent the name Snow White.

HUHU ... A word meaning angry.

HILAHILA ... The Hawaiian word for bashful.

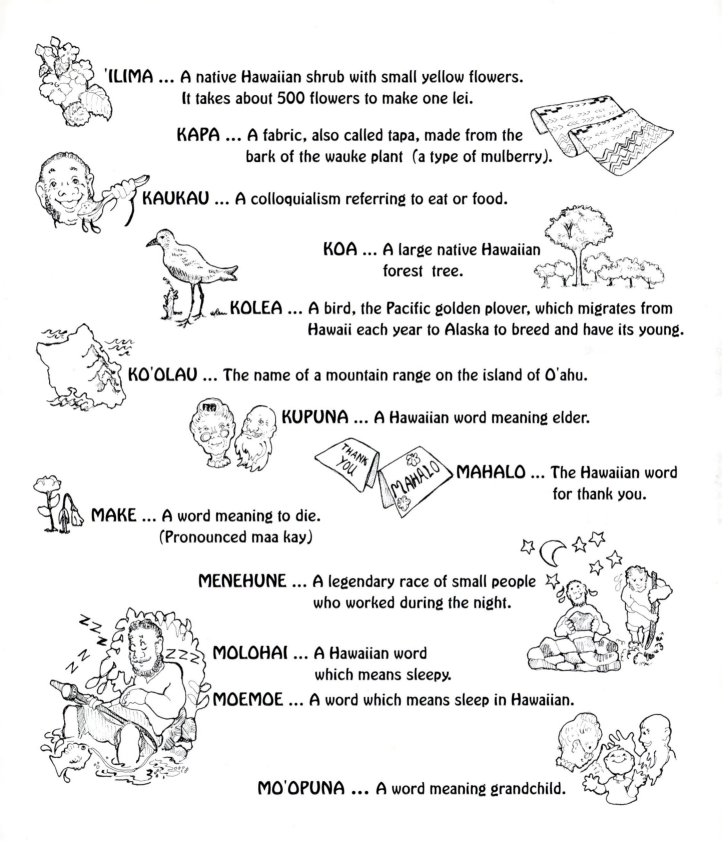

'ILIMA ... A native Hawaiian shrub with small yellow flowers. It takes about 500 flowers to make one lei.

KAPA ... A fabric, also called tapa, made from the bark of the wauke plant (a type of mulberry).

KAUKAU ... A colloquialism referring to eat or food.

KOA ... A large native Hawaiian forest tree.

KOLEA ... A bird, the Pacific golden plover, which migrates from Hawaii each year to Alaska to breed and have its young.

KO'OLAU ... The name of a mountain range on the island of O'ahu.

KUPUNA ... A Hawaiian word meaning elder.

MAHALO ... The Hawaiian word for thank you.

MAKE ... A word meaning to die. (Pronounced maa kay)

MENEHUNE ... A legendary race of small people who worked during the night.

MOLOHAI ... A Hawaiian word which means sleepy.

MOEMOE ... A word which means sleep in Hawaiian.

MO'OPUNA ... A word meaning grandchild.

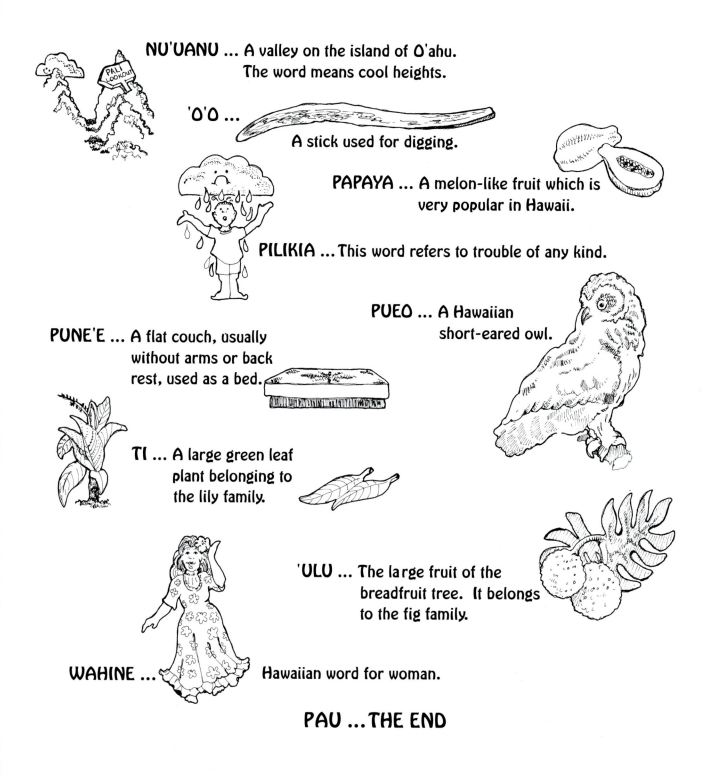

NU'UANU ... A valley on the island of O'ahu. The word means cool heights.

'O'O ... A stick used for digging.

PAPAYA ... A melon-like fruit which is very popular in Hawaii.

PILIKIA ... This word refers to trouble of any kind.

PUEO ... A Hawaiian short-eared owl.

PUNE'E ... A flat couch, usually without arms or back rest, used as a bed.

TI ... A large green leaf plant belonging to the lily family.

'ULU ... The large fruit of the breadfruit tree. It belongs to the fig family.

WAHINE ... Hawaiian word for woman.

PAU ... THE END